Wishbone

WRITTEN AND ILLUSTRATED BY

Barbara Williamson

To order additional copies of this book, contact:
Xlibris
1-888-795-4274
www.Xlibris.com
Orders@Xlibris.com

ISBN:	Softcover	978-1-4363-4277-3
	EBook	978-1-4771-8125-6

Print information available on the last page

Rev. date: 05/18/2020

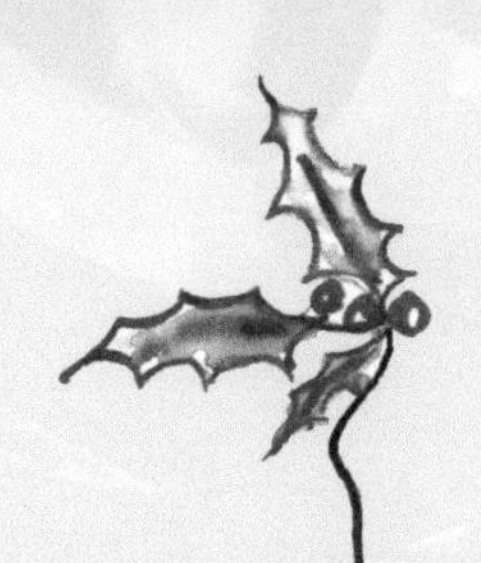

Thank you, Derek, Kelly, Danielle, and Kimberly.
I love you so.
You fill my life with stories.
Love to Kara, Trevor, and Patrick –
my children, too, as of
March 28, 1999.

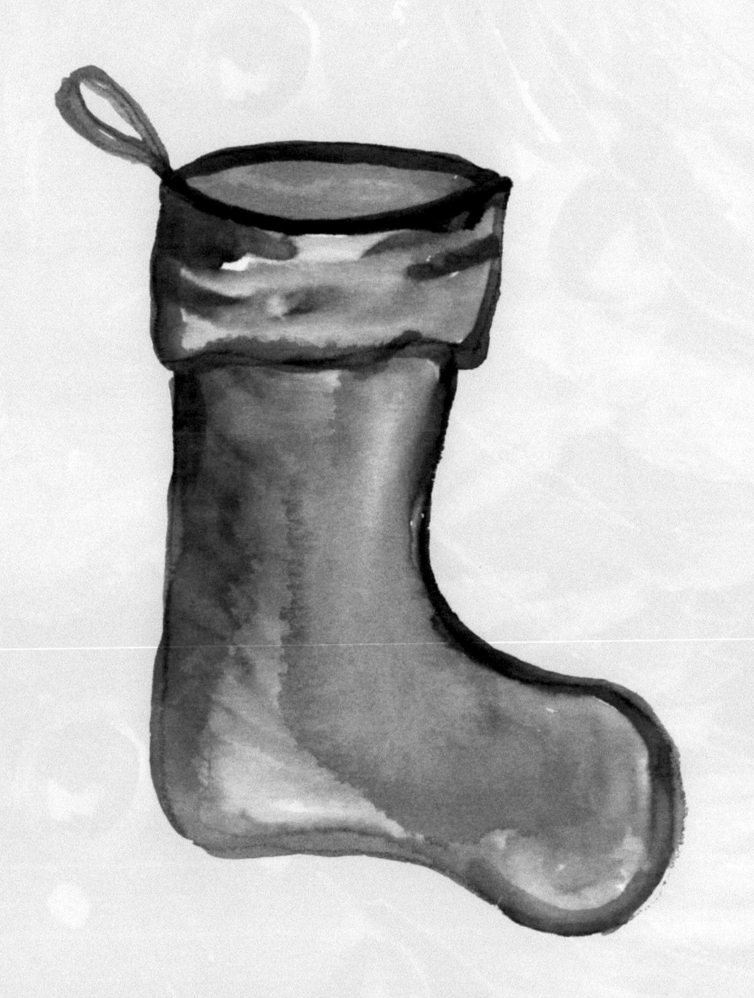

Hi, my name is Danielle. I am four years old and I have a sister. Her name is Kimberly, but sometimes I call her Sissy. We are both very excited, because there are only two weeks until Christmas. I keep wishing Christmas was tomorrow.

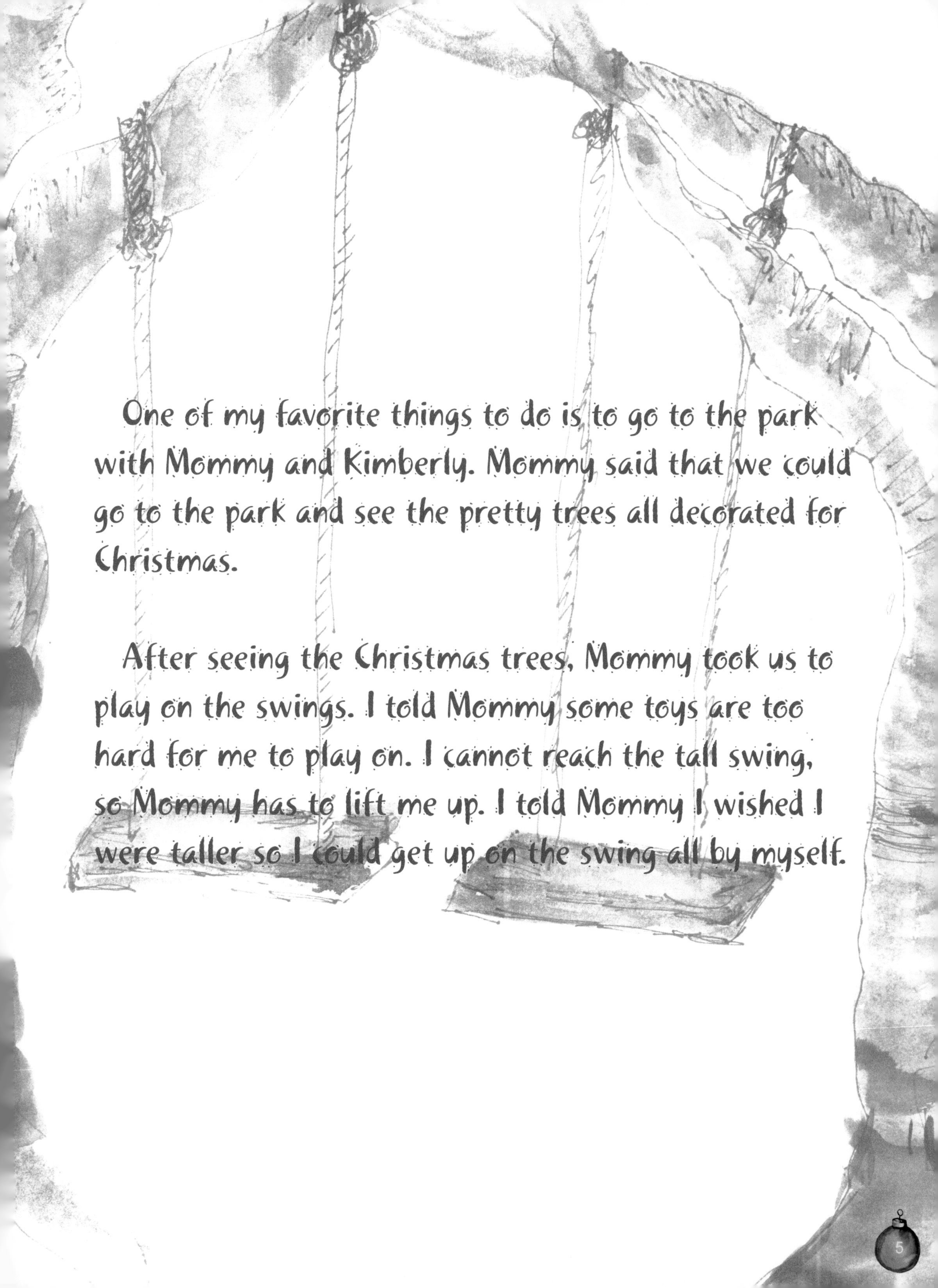

One of my favorite things to do is to go to the park with Mommy and Kimberly. Mommy said that we could go to the park and see the pretty trees all decorated for Christmas.

After seeing the Christmas trees, Mommy took us to play on the swings. I told Mommy some toys are too hard for me to play on. I cannot reach the tall swing, so Mommy has to lift me up. I told Mommy I wished I were taller so I could get up on the swing all by myself.

"Oh, Danielle, do not wish your life away," Mommy said.

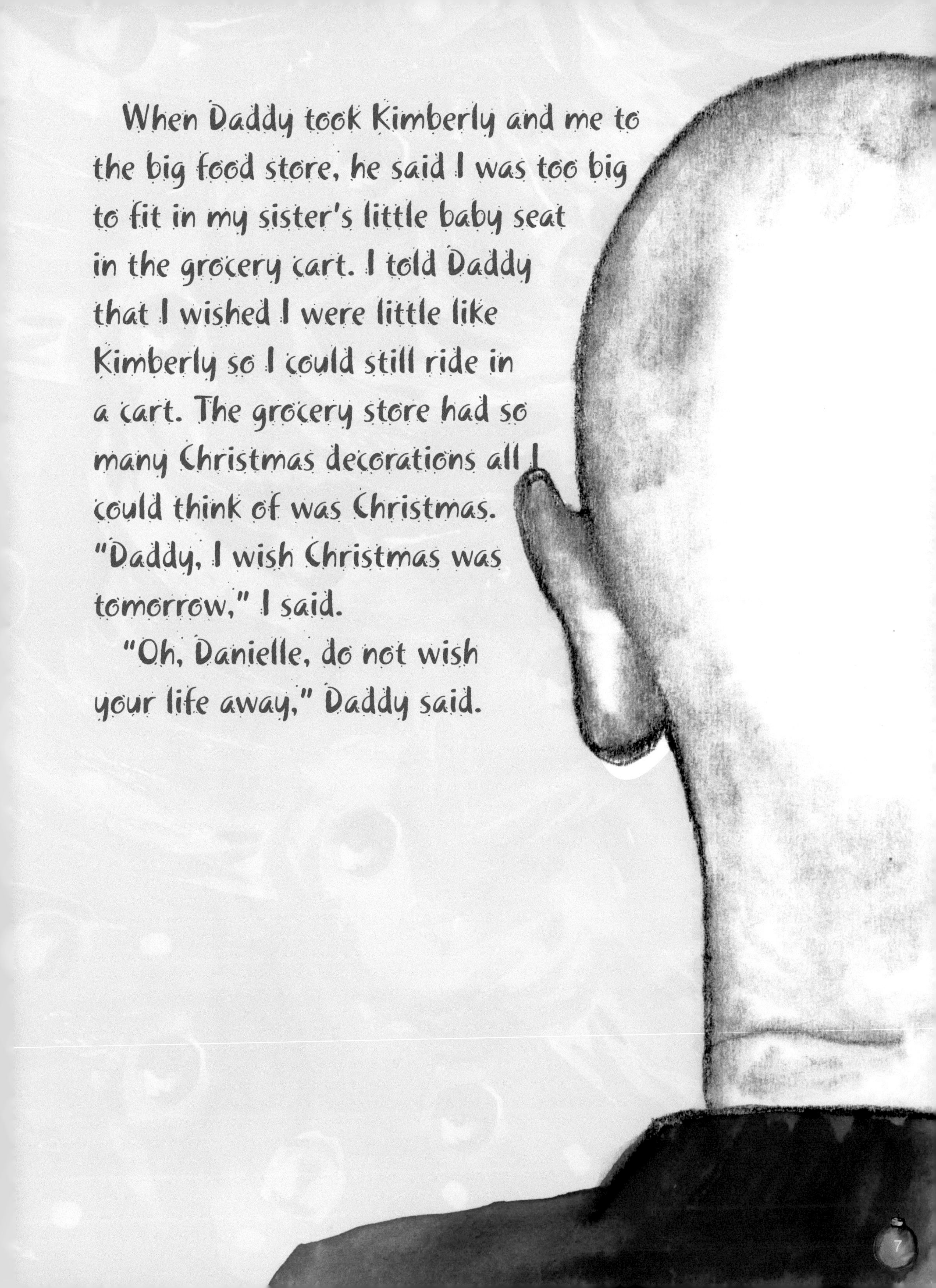

When Daddy took Kimberly and me to the big food store, he said I was too big to fit in my sister's little baby seat in the grocery cart. I told Daddy that I wished I were little like Kimberly so I could still ride in a cart. The grocery store had so many Christmas decorations all I could think of was Christmas. "Daddy, I wish Christmas was tomorrow," I said.

"Oh, Danielle, do not wish your life away," Daddy said.

The next day, Mommy took Kimberly and me to the zoo. Mommy asked if I wanted to ride in the stroller with Kimberly. I said, "I wish I didn't have to ride in a stroller like a little baby." "Okay Miss Danielle, this wish will come true. You can walk while your sister rides," said Mommy.

We saw a huge Christmas tree and I wished we could have one that big at our house. Then we saw seals and I wished I could swim all day. "Look, Mommy. There are some giraffes! I wish I had a long neck like a giraffe. Then I could see over the tops of the Christmas trees," I said. "Wish, wish, and wish! Oh, Danielle, you are wishing your life away again," Mommy said.

I was beginning to get tired of walking and I wished I had listened to Mommy and rode in the stroller with Kimberly. I said to Mommy, "I wish I could sit by my sister." She replied, "Danielle, I thought you were a big girl who wanted to walk." I said, "Well, now I wish I could ride."

"Oh, Danielle," Mommy said, "you and your wishing!"

Then she helped me into the stroller and said, "Danielle, Daddy and I have told you about wishing your life away."

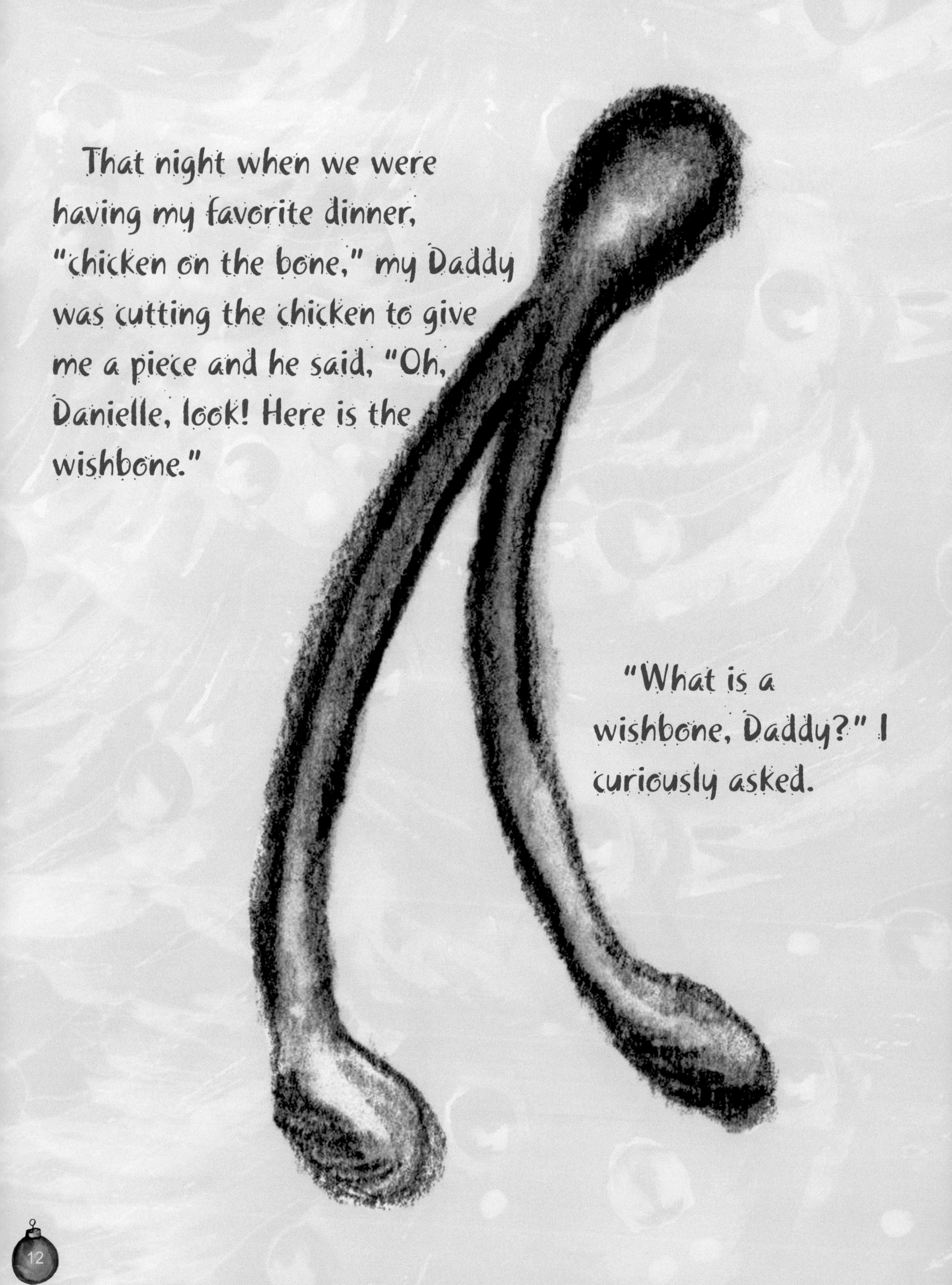

That night when we were having my favorite dinner, "chicken on the bone," my Daddy was cutting the chicken to give me a piece and he said, "Oh, Danielle, look! Here is the wishbone."

"What is a wishbone, Daddy?" I curiously asked.

Danielle, I'm surprised you do not know what a wishbone is." He showed me the wishbone and said, "This, my sweet Danielle, is the wishbone. The reason it is called a wishbone is because two people take hold of an end and pull, and when it breaks, the person with the biggest half is the winner and gets to make a wish."

"Oh, Daddy, I wish I could have the wishbone!" I exclaimed.

"Since you are always making wishes, maybe Mommy and I should call you Wishbone, Danielle. Here you go, Wishbone, this one is for you," Daddy said. "Why don't you put this in a special place and keep it for a special wish?" he added lovingly.

After dinner, I went to my bedroom and put the wishbone in my treasure box, which is under a paper Christmas tree that I made at school.

The next morning I was feeling hot and sick. When Mommy felt my head, she told me we needed to go to the doctor's office. I like to see the doctor. His name is Doctor Syd and he helps me feel better.

Doctor Syd told us I had a fever; it was not very high, but I should rest so I would be all-better before Christmas. I told him my new, funny name was Wishbone.

"You must mean nickname, Danielle," the doctor said. "Why is that your nickname?" he asked.

Mommy told the doctor I am wishing all the time, and she and Daddy keep telling me to stop wishing my life away.

I told the doctor I was wishing I could ride in an ambulance. He looked at Mommy, shook his head, and said, "I see what you mean. Let me think on this a while and I will call you."

A couple of days later the doctor called. He wanted Mommy and Daddy to bring me to the hospital. Kimberly stayed at my grandma's house because she is too little to go to the hospital. He said he had something to show us and to meet him in front of the doors marked "Children's Section." He told Mommy they would be easy to find because they had Christmas wreaths on the windows.

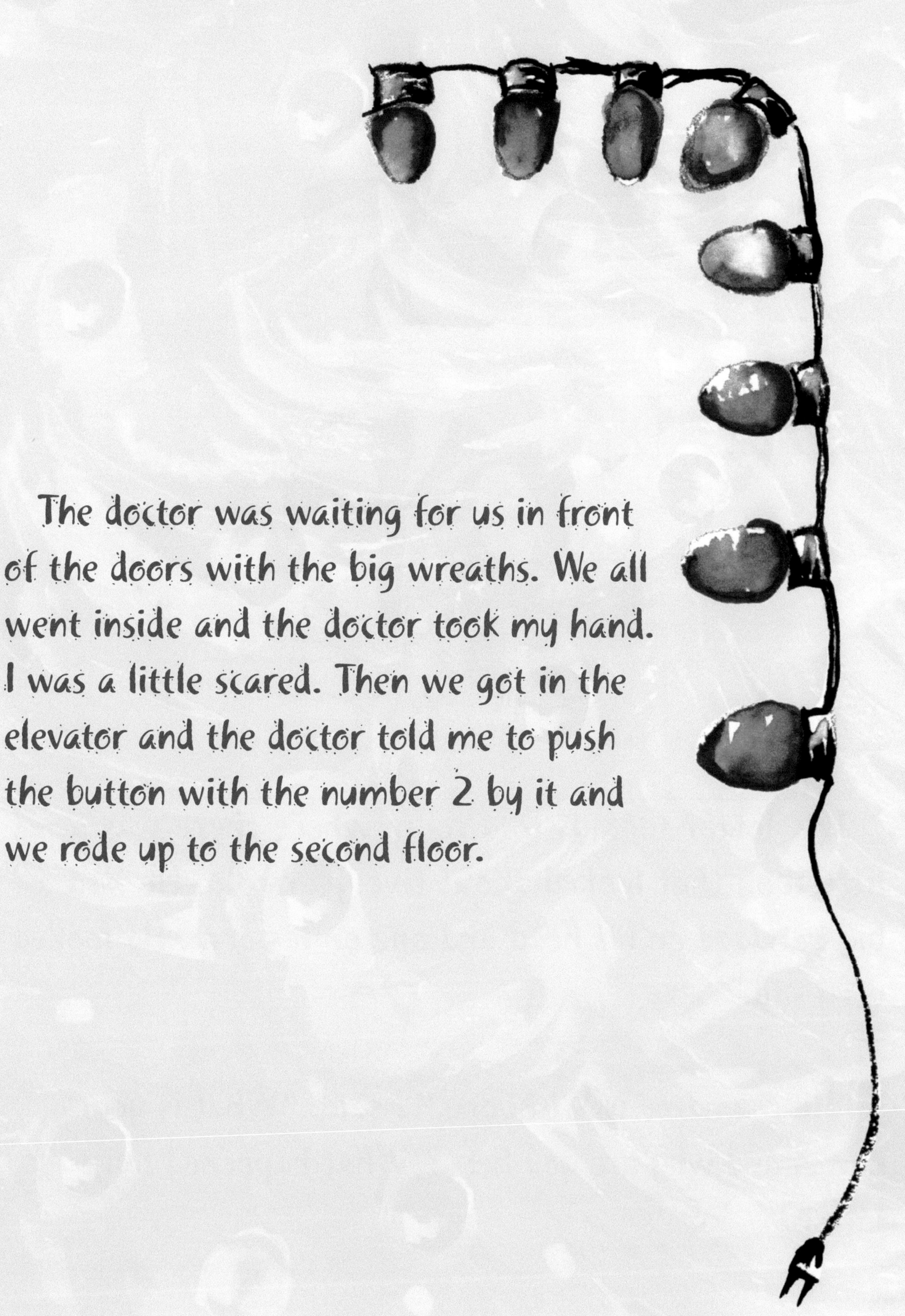

The doctor was waiting for us in front of the doors with the big wreaths. We all went inside and the doctor took my hand. I was a little scared. Then we got in the elevator and the doctor told me to push the button with the number 2 by it and we rode up to the second floor.

The doctor took us to a room where there was a little boy that looked about five years old. He had a big bandage on his head and one on his arm. He looked very sad.

"Hi, my name is Wishbone," I said. "What is your name, and why are you here? What happened to you?" I asked.

"My name is Trevor," he replied. "I jumped off my bed and hurt my arm and head. I was just wishing I could fly. Boy, was I wrong! Now, I just wish that I can be home by Christmas," he said sadly.

"Wishbone, we'd better let Trevor rest. We have two more stops to make," the doctor said. We told Trevor goodbye and left his room.

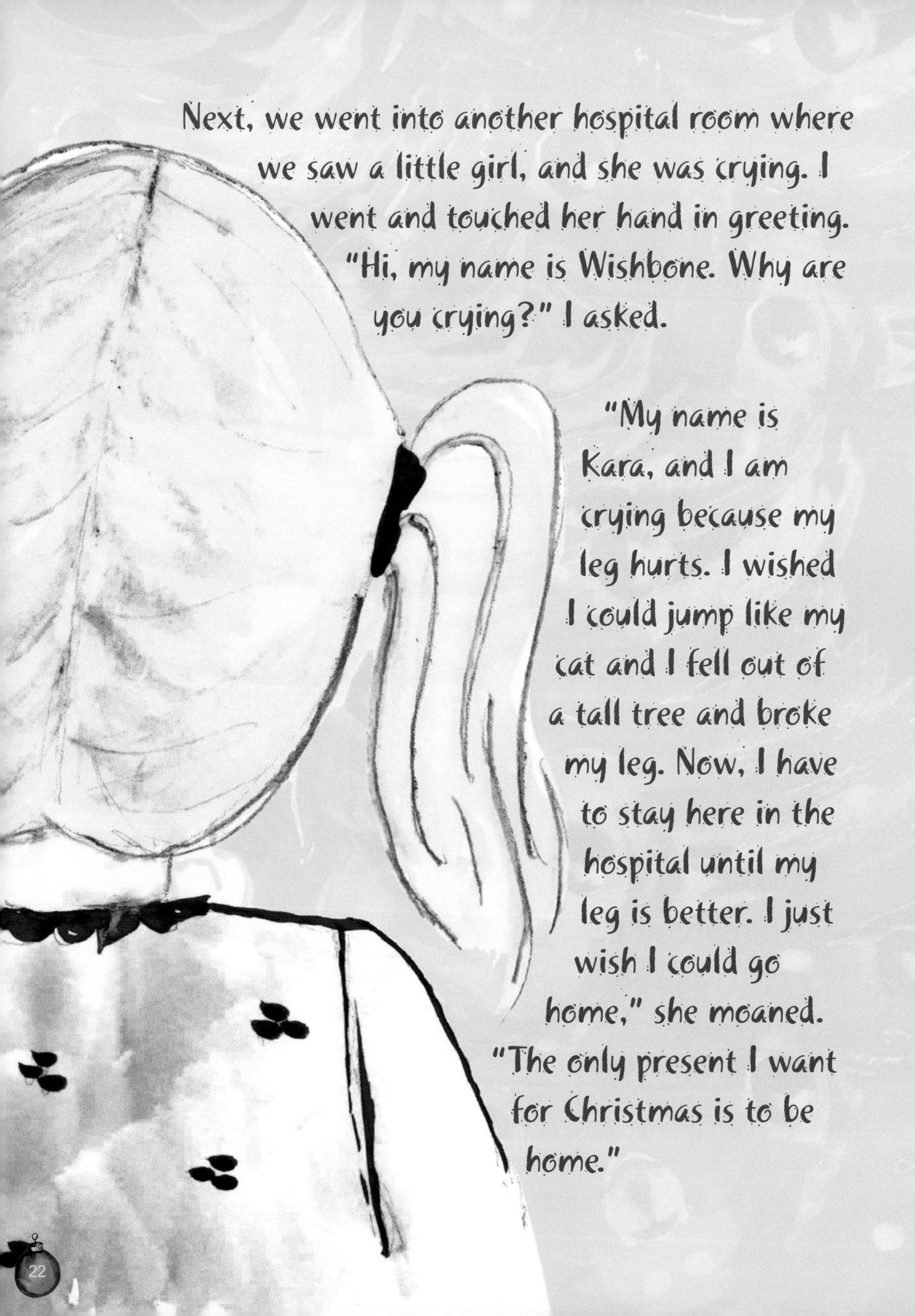

Next, we went into another hospital room where we saw a little girl, and she was crying. I went and touched her hand in greeting. "Hi, my name is Wishbone. Why are you crying?" I asked.

"My name is Kara, and I am crying because my leg hurts. I wished I could jump like my cat and I fell out of a tall tree and broke my leg. Now, I have to stay here in the hospital until my leg is better. I just wish I could go home," she moaned. "The only present I want for Christmas is to be home."

"Come on, Wishbone. We have one more visit to make. Say goodbye to Kara," the doctor whispered. We said goodbye and walked down the hall to our last stop.

There, we walked into a room where there was a boy that had big bandages all over his arms. "What happened to this boy, doctor?" I asked.

"Why don't you ask Patrick what happened?" replied the doctor.

Patrick started to cry and told us he just wished he could make rockets with old firecrackers, but they exploded and burned his arms badly. I learned my lesson playing with fire and firecrackers," Patrick noted. "I am all done playing with fire and firecrackers," Patrick said humbly. "I wish I could go home for Christmas. Oh! I mean I sure hope I can go home for Christmas."

On Christmas Eve, Mommy served dinner and I was not very hungry. I asked if I could be excused for just a minute. I went to my bedroom and got my special treasure box and I brought it back to the table.

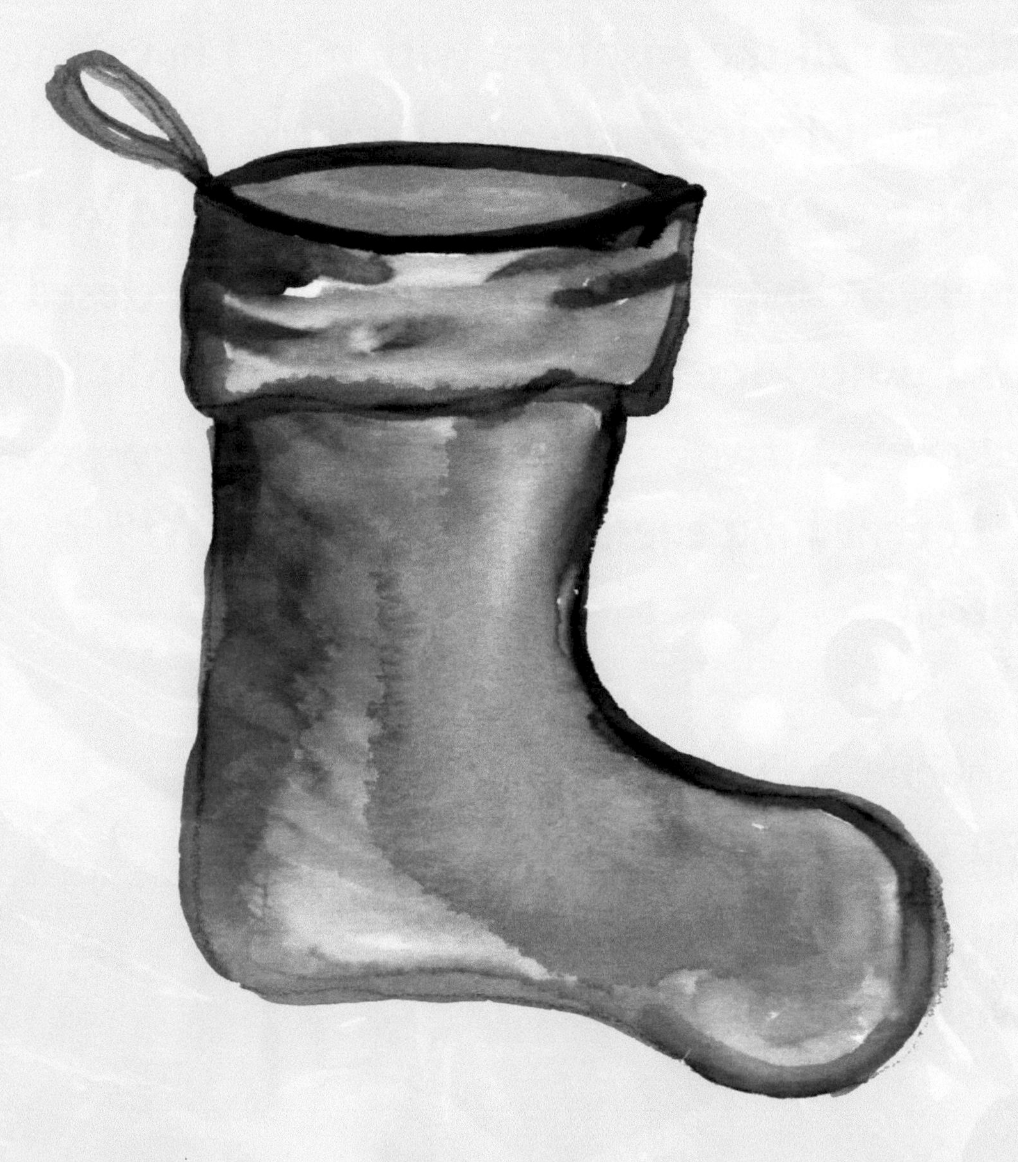

Daddy said, "What did you bring your special box to the table for, Wishbone?"

"Daddy, will you do something special with me?" I asked.

"Of course I will," he replied. "What would you like me to do?"

"Will you pull the wishbone with me? I have a very special wish if I win," I answered, taking the wishbone out of the treasure box. "Okay Daddy," I said as I put my fingers around my side of the wishbone, closed my eyes, and waited for Daddy to hold his side. My Mommy counted one . . . two . . . three! I waited a few seconds before I opened my eyes, "OH! I won! WOW!" I exclaimed.

"Wishbone, you won," Mommy said. "Will you tell Mommy and Daddy your wish?" she added.

"I guess, since it really is about you and Daddy, I'd better tell you," I said. I stood up straight and tall, and happily said, "Mommy, Daddy

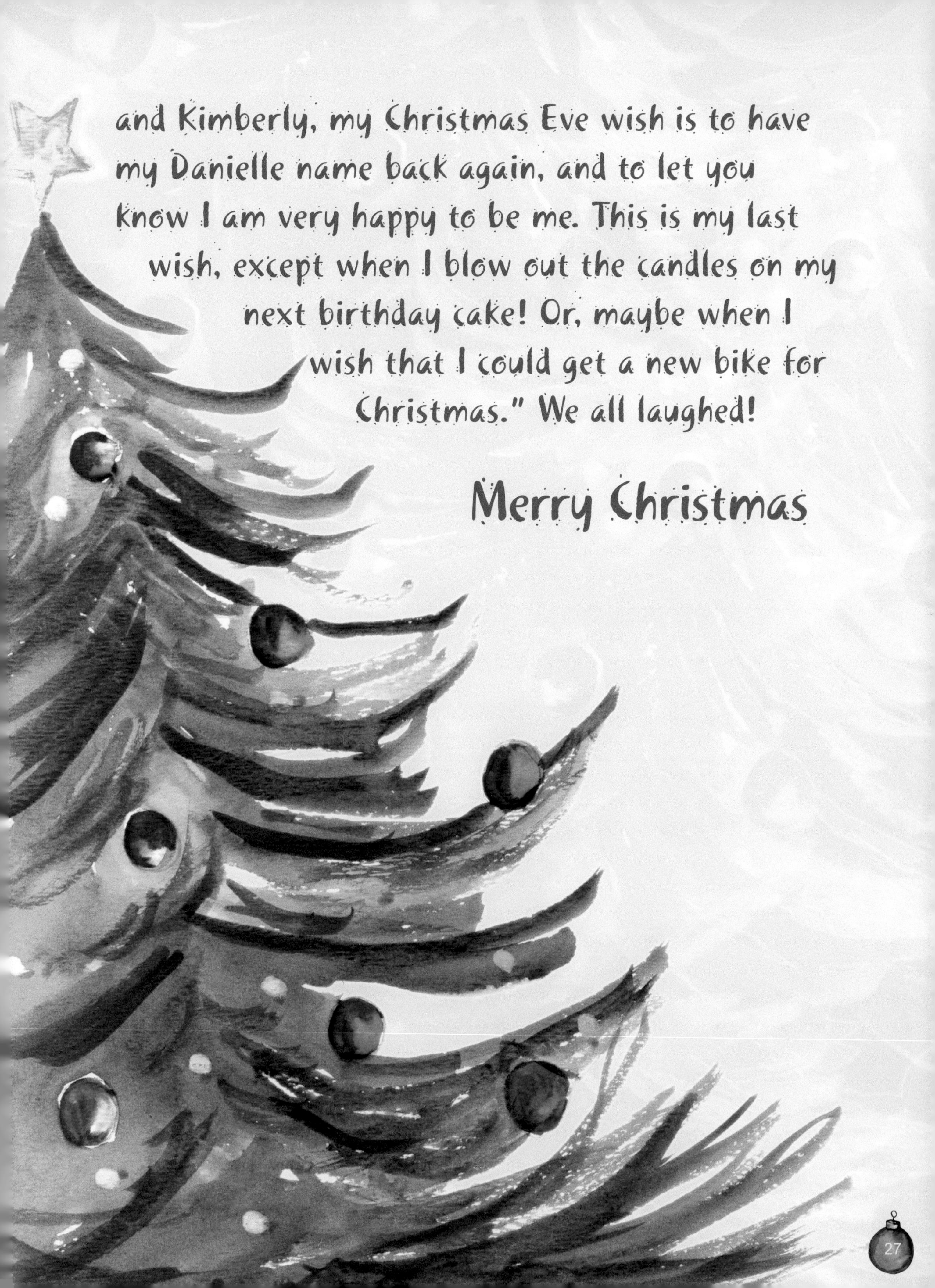

and Kimberly, my Christmas Eve wish is to have my Danielle name back again, and to let you know I am very happy to be me. This is my last wish, except when I blow out the candles on my next birthday cake! Or, maybe when I wish that I could get a new bike for Christmas." We all laughed!

Merry Christmas